ONIKA

WWW.AUTHORBRIJONES.COM

Bri Jones

Onika is a work of fiction. Names, characters, places, and incidents are the products of the author's imagination or are used fictitiously. Any resemblance to actual events, locales, or persons, living or dead, is entirely coincidental.

Published in the United States by Bri Jones.

ISBN-10: 099647024
ISBN-13: 978-0-9964702-0-9

Printed in the United States of America
brijones128@gmail.com

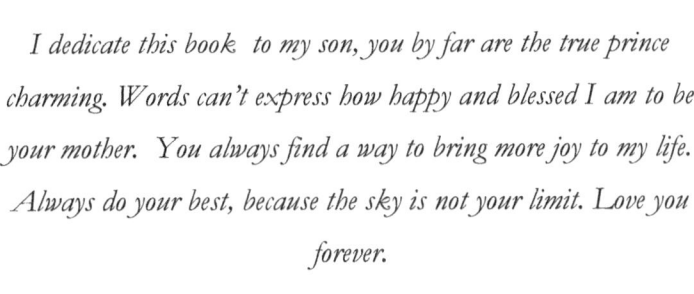

I dedicate this book to my son, you by far are the true prince charming. Words can't express how happy and blessed I am to be your mother. You always find a way to bring more joy to my life. Always do your best, because the sky is not your limit. Love you forever.

Acknowledgment

First and foremost, I want to thank God for the vision and imagination to write this book. I also thank my wonderful son for his patience, motivation and encouragement to achieve my goals. My son keeps me smiling. My son is my inspiration for continuing to improve my knowledge and advance my career.

I'd like to thank my brother for proofreading and brainstorming with me to develop new ideas for this book. I'd like to thank my parents, brothers, friends and additional family for their continuous support in all my different journeys.

Again, thanks to all my family and friends for sharing my excitement in starting this venture and their continuous encouragement when I became discouraged in completing this book. Thank you to my editor, Tracy Scott and book cover designer, David Martinez on their time and hard work. Lastly, I want to thank you, the readers, for your support in purchasing my book. Everyone's support is greatly appreciated.

CHAPTER ONE

In the beautiful land of Africa was one of the largest and most prestigious kingdoms, known as Zalaya. Zalaya was led by the highly respected and loved King Mateo and Queen Cecilia. They had a beautiful, intelligent and vigorous daughter, named Princess Onika. Princess Onika was not like the average Princess; she was very adventurous, outgoing, often humorous and most of all, she had the biggest heart anyone could be known to have. Everyone who interacted with the Princess grew to love her instantly because of her genuine and kind spirit. The Princess had a beautiful smile that could light up anyone's rainy day and a voice that could warm your soul. The Princess had sparkling hazel eyes and curly, long, thick, dark reddish brown hair. The Princess had a distinguished sense of fashion that she enjoyed displaying in her custom jewelry, clothes, hair and other accessories. Princess Onika often shared her many talents and creativity with the children and young adults of her kingdom. Princess Onika also spent a lot of time with the elders of her kingdom, listening to stories and learning from their wisdom. Princess Onika did not do these things to just gain the respect and loyalty of her citizens, it was because she truly enjoyed the time and experiences she shared with everyone. Princess Onika possessed a joyful spirit and often shared it through her singing and humming as she walked or danced throughout the kingdom yards. Princess Onika brought calmness to her father whenever he heard her sing.

In the Zalaya kingdom, as well as many other kingdoms in Africa, was the traditional arranged marriage ceremony that was just eight months away for Princess Onika. Princess Onika would meet her future husband for the first time during the traditional marriage ceremony that would take place in eight months. Traditionally, the King would lead in the process of selecting the Prince and together the King and Queen would agree on the final decision. This was a highly honored traditional ceremony that many leaders of other kingdoms would attend. Princess Onika was never fond of this tradition and had often given her parents a hard time about going through with this ceremony. Princess Onika felt that she should be able to pick her own husband or at least be a part of the process. Unfortunately, King Mateo was firm about upholding the honor of the tradition because it had been implemented successfully for many centuries. Onika could only hope that she and her husband could experience the same love that her parents share.

The Zalaya kingdom was well known for its Annual Festival Celebration, which included music, dancing, artwork, talent shows, custom dishes from throughout the kingdom and many other events that lasted for seven days. Those from numerous kingdoms throughout Africa would attend this annual festival celebration and present gifts in honor of the King, Queen and Princess. This festival celebration was one of Princess Onika's favorite times of year. It was an opportunity for Onika to meet new people and be involved in all the activities.

Princess Onika began to get prepared for the first day of the festival. She felt like she couldn't get dressed quick enough to get out the palace doors to start enjoying the activities. Princess Onika always enjoyed being actively involved in the festival, interacting with the guests and meeting new people from the different kingdoms. During the first couple of days of the festival, Princess Onika greeted as many guests as she could get to and helped the citizens of Zalaya setup their store displays and games for the visitors and guests. Princess Onika also made sure to purchase some accessories to add to her collection and taste the custom homemade dishes.

On the third day of the festival, while the citizens performed their traditional dance segment, Princess Onika was approached by a handsome man who wanted to dance. His name was Prince Ezra from the fourth largest kingdom of Africa and this was his first time attending Zalaya's Annual Festival Celebration. Princess Onika and Prince Ezra danced for hours, which to them felt like timeless seconds. During a break in the dancing, they began to walk around the festival yard and enjoy some of the specialized dishes and other entertainment. The Prince and Princess toured the festival yard for hours enjoying each other's company. They shared many stories and laughs as they enjoyed different attractions at the festival. As the citizens of Zalaya began to prepare for the final dance segment prior to the festival ending for the night, Prince Ezra and Princess Onika began to walk toward the dancers.

From the palace stage the King kept a close visual on the Princess and her new friend, the Prince. The King was not pleased with the close interaction between the Princess and the Prince, so the King sent a servant to retrieve the Princess promptly to interrupt further involvement. As the servant approached the Princess to inform her of the King's immediate request of her presence, the Prince quickly grabbed a single rose from the closest table. As the Prince presented the Princess with the rose, he kissed her hand and told the Princess he would return before the festival celebration ended on the last day. When Princess Onika reached the room where her father was impatiently waiting for her, the King immediately excused everyone in the room to talk to his daughter in private. Before the Princess could say anything, the King demanded that the Princess never see the Prince again. In a disappointing tone the King stated, "Have you forgotten that you are to get married in eight months?" The King continued to inform the Princess of all the time and efforts he put into selecting the best Prince he felt would be most suitable for her to marry and help lead the kingdom one day. The Queen suggested that the Princess was simply having innocent fun with the Prince. (The Princess thought to herself that even though their interaction was innocent, she really liked the Prince as more than just a friend). The King replied, "It doesn't look good having the Princess parading around the festival yard in that manner with another Prince especially since the official announcement has gone forward of the upcoming traditional marriage ceremony. It's not a favorable image for the Princess or for both kingdoms involved." As King Mateo spoke, Princess Onika's mind often drifted away thinking about Prince Ezra, but she knew she had to detain her smile to prevent further frustrating her father. As Princess Onika was excused by her father and walked toward her room, she couldn't help but smile from all the thoughts of the magical day she had with Prince Ezra.

Prince Ezra knew from the first interaction with Princess Onika she was meant to be his Queen. Prince Ezra had never been so mesmerized by any Princess before, but there was something special about Princess Onika. Prince Ezra couldn't decide if it was Onika's beautiful smile, sparkling hazel eyes or long reddish hair that captivated him the most. Prince Ezra loved her personality, sense of humor and the sound of her laughter. Prince Ezra could tell Princess Onika was a kind and caring person by her interaction with the citizens of her kingdom. When Prince Ezra returned to his kingdom, he couldn't wait to tell his younger brother, Omar, about Princess Onika. Prince Omar was happy to hear that his brother met someone he really liked, but he didn't have the same appreciation for Princess Onika as Prince Ezra hoped for. Prince Omar was more focused on sports and other activities than anything else. Prince Ezra wanted to also tell his best friend, Prince Ramir, but as their responsibilities for their respective kingdoms grew more demanding they didn't have much time to hang out. Prince Ezra and Prince Ramir met over 10 years ago at summer training and instantly became inseparable. They fought and argued like brothers, but they always found a way to reconcile their differences.

On day four of the festival celebration, Princess

Onika headed toward the palace doors and the King requested her presence, now. King Mateo reminded his daughter of their conversation yesterday and the Princess replied that she understood. Princess Onika continued her activities as normal throughout the festival yards with the citizens and guests. Although the Princess knew what her father told her, she still was hoping to see Prince Ezra again. As the festival day ended, the Princess was kind of disappointed not to see Prince Ezra, but she knew there were still three more days left of the festival celebration.

For three days, Princess Onika anticipated Prince Ezra's return, growing discouraged that she would never see her Prince charming again. As Prince Ezra promised, toward the end of the last day of the festival, he returned to the Zalaya kingdom. Shortly upon Prince Ezra's arrival, Princess Onika spotted him and instantly became excited! The Princess knew she had to find a way to talk to the Prince without drawing her father's attention. The King made himself clear to his daughter that she was forbidden from speaking or having any further interaction with the Prince again. Princess Onika always enjoyed taking the occasional risk; however, she never dishonored her parents in such a manner. Princess Onika lived for the ultimate approval of both her parents, but especially her father. Even though she didn't want to disappoint them, Princess Onika's heart could not just let her do nothing.

Princess Onika was able to discreetly leave the King's side and race to her room to change into clothes that were a little less conspicuous. Once Princess Onika reached the festival yard, she located Prince Ezra. Princess Onika was able to draw Prince Ezra's attention without causing any commotion. The Princess directed the Prince to a secluded area where they could talk briefly. Princess Onika told Prince Ezra she wanted to continue seeing him after the festival ended. Prince Ezra was glad to hear that because he felt the same. They both made plans to reunite right outside the kingdom yards after the Princess completed her routine visits to the elder citizens of her kingdom. Princess Onika knew that her visits varied with the elder citizens, so it wouldn't be suspicious to her parents if she were late returning to the palace.

Princess Onika and Prince Ezra met as planned outside the kingdom entrance and then rode out a little

further until they found a good location. The location
they found was a narrow opening of the forest by a
river called Pearl. The area was filled with colorful
plants, trees and flowers. Princess Onika was very
nervous meeting Prince Ezra the first day because all
she could hear was her father's voice forbidding her to
see him again. As they rode their horses around the
open yards, the voice of her father began to fade.
Prince Ezra was a very pleasant, funny and strong
gentleman. Princess Onika really enjoyed his company.
It seemed like they never ran out of things to talk
about. They shared stories about their kingdoms,
families, friends and things about themselves. They
had a lot of things in common: they both enjoyed
helping people, riding horses, playing sports, exploring
new tropical forests outside of their respective
kingdoms and having fun with family and friends.
Often when Prince Ezra and Princess Onika would
meet they would race on their horses through the
woods to see who would find their way out first. They
would take long walks to explore new areas or they
would simply sit on the grass to talk and share laughs.
Meeting each other was the highlight of their days and
they enjoyed each other's company so much they never

wanted to leave each other. Saying bye at the end of each evening was always the hardest part.

Three months had quickly passed since Princess Onika and Prince Ezra first met at the festival. The once innocent friendship was growing more and more into an emotional connection. The Princess continued to dread more and more the upcoming marriage ceremony. Princess Onika decided to express the feelings that she developed for Prince Ezra and he confirmed that he felt the same way for her. Princess Onika was also reluctant to inform Prince Ezra of her upcoming arranged marriage ceremony in a few months. Disturbed by what Princess Onika was telling him, Prince Ezra was not surprised because he was very familiar with the traditional arranged marriage ceremonies that were implemented throughout many of the kingdoms in Africa. As their evening together came to an end, Prince Ezra softly kissed Princess Onika on her forehead and quietly suggested that this evening conclude them seeing each other again. As Prince Ezra stood, he reached for Princess Onika's hand to help her to her feet then kissed her hand and told her, "You will forever be in my heart."

Princess Onika's heart did not want to say bye to her first love, but the Princess knew it would only make things more complicated if they continued to see each other. Fighting her urge to stop him from leaving, Princess Onika sadly blew Prince Ezra a kiss and waved farewell. It was hard for Prince Ezra to walk away and know that he may not ever see Princess Onika again. Prince Ezra knew he had to be strong because as time passed it wouldn't get any easier. As tears ran down Princess Onika's face, she gathered her things and started her journey back to the palace.

Princess Onika entered the palace and went straight to her room trying to avoid any contact with anyone. Normally, when the Princess would return from one of her excursions, she would tell her parents all about it, but her meetings with the Prince were the exception, of course. This made it obvious to King Mateo and Queen Cecilia that something was troubling the Princess. King Mateo went to Princess Onika's room to check on her and make sure everything was okay. King Mateo wanted reassurance that everything went smoothly during Princess Onika's visits to the elder citizens of the kingdom. Princess Onika assured her father that everything went well; however, she just needed some time by herself. A bit confused, King Mateo left Princess Onika's room. As King Mateo returned back to Queen Cecilia, she inquired about the outcome of his brief visit with their daughter. The King did not have an answer for the Queen, but he knew something was not right. King Mateo and Queen Cecilia decided to let the Princess rest and then the Queen would check on her again the following day if nothing changes.

The next day, the King and Queen observed the Princess's behavior during breakfast and throughout the day. Princess Onika's behavior was slightly better than the previous day; however, she still was not quite herself. Princess Onika tried her hardest to portray her normal and upbeat behavior around the palace but the truth was she was heartbroken. Princess Onika knew she couldn't talk to her parents about it because she was forbidden to see Prince Ezra again during the festival. As agreed, later that evening Queen Cecilia visited Princess Onika's room to check on her. Princess Onika knew she had to furnish her mother with a good justification for the changes in her

13

behavior, so they would stop inquiring. As Queen Cecilia brushed and braided Princess Onika's hair, Queen Cecilia expressed her concerns of Princess Onika's behavior over the last couple days. Princess Onika didn't want to lie but she knew she couldn't tell her mother that her heart was broken either. So the Princess replied that she was not ready to get married and was very nervous. (Princess Onika felt that disclosure was a compromise because it was true, but not the whole truth). Queen Cecilia asked, "Are you sure there isn't more?" Princess Onika paused and replied, "No, mother, that's why." Queen Cecilia tried to give Princess Onika some encouraging words to help her cope with her feelings. The Queen also shared that she felt the same way prior to marrying Onika's father. They took the time to get to know each other and soon they both fell deeply in love with each other. The Queen added that she wouldn't trade the King for another in the world. Queen Cecilia assured Princess Onika that sometimes you have to trust your parents' judgment and decisions, because their life experience and wisdom could result in a happier and more successful life in the long term. This gave Princess Onika slight hope for her upcoming marriage.

CHAPTER TWO

I t was one day away from the marriage ceremony and the union of the two kingdoms, Queen Cecilia helped Princess Onika with her final preparations for the ceremony. The ceremony would be held in a central location between the two kingdoms. Princess Onika was very nervous about meeting her future husband for the first time, but she knew this was what she was destined to do. Princess Onika couldn't help but to think about Prince Ezra as she stared to the sky out the palace window. The Princess wondered what the Prince was doing and whether he ever thought about her. Princess Onika never stopped thinking about Prince Ezra. She often dreamt about all the excitement they had together and one day being reunited. Queen Cecilia quietly walked beside her daughter and wrapped her arms around the Princess with a big hug. Princess Onika turned slightly to embrace her mother's hug by laying her head on the Queen's chest. The Princess told her mother, "You always give the best hugs to make everything feel better." The Queen assured her daughter everything would be fine and with an open mind she would find happiness with her future husband.

During the early afternoon, the citizens of Zalaya hosted a parade in honor of Princess Onika. The parade consisted of drummers, dancers, confetti, flags, artifacts, balloons and many other symbols to show the love and respect the citizens of Zalaya have for their Princess. Following the parade was a talent show hosted by the young adults of the kingdom, which the Princess had a major positive impact on. As the celebration came to a close and night began to fall, the Queen suggested that everyone get to bed early because of the eventful day they had awaiting them in the morning.

Bright and early, the sounds of the trumpets filled the air as the sun ascended throughout the kingdom of Zalaya. The King, Queen and Princess gathered around the table to have breakfast and enjoy brief conversations before getting ready for the ceremony. Before leaving the table, Queen Cecilia presented Princess Onika with a beautiful flower hairpin; it was the same pin she wore at their wedding. King Mateo then gave Princess Onika dazzling earrings that his mother wore at her wedding. Princess Onika was ecstatic by her parents' heartfelt gifts. Princess Onika embraced both of her parents tightly and thanked them for their sincere gifts. King Mateo kissed the Queen and his daughter and expressed how much he cherished them both very dearly and how proud he was of Princess Onika.

Princess Onika was escorted by her parents to a silver, white and blue carriage that waited outside the palace. Traditionally, the Queen would ride with the Princess to the ceremony but Princess Onika requested to ride alone. Queen Cecilia did not dispute Princess Onika's request and returned to the carriage behind to accompany King Mateo. The ride to the ceremony was full of beautiful sights of animals, plants, tropical forests and waterfalls. Princess Onika tried not to think about Prince Ezra and focus on the life she was about to begin with her future husband. Princess Onika was finally at peace with the marriage ceremony and was convinced that one day she would grow to have the same love with her husband that her parents share. Princess Onika knew she was doing the best thing for her kingdom. They arrived to the ceremony and King Mateo and Queen Cecilia led Princess Onika to the ceremony doors. Before Queen Cecilia was ushered to the front of the ceremony, she turned to Princess Onika to assure she was okay. Princess Onika released a beautiful big smile and persuaded her mother everything was fine. Right before walking down the aisle, King Mateo looked at Princess Onika and told her how proud he was to have her as a daughter.

As Princess Onika walked down the aisle with her father to meet her future husband, she felt confident that she was doing the right thing. As King Mateo and Princess Onika were getting closer, she could see her handsome and strong future husband standing there waiting patiently to take her hand. Princess Onika glanced into the crowd only to make eye contact with Prince Ezra. Prince Ezra was standing close to the front, which signified that he knew her future husband personally. Princess Onika began to panic feeling a shortness of breath and slight dizziness. She clutched her father's arm to remain balanced, as her legs grew weaker the more steps she took. The King whispered to the Princess, "The hard part is almost over. Just take a deep breath." As Princess Onika got closer to the altar and began to walk pass where Prince Ezra was standing, tears raced down her face and her hands began to shake. King Mateo whispered to the Princess, "Please do not embarrass us or the kingdom; you can do this. It's your destiny." As the King released his arm from the Princess, he replaced it with the arm of her future husband Prince Ramir.

Princess Onika did not want to shame her parents, but the more the minster continued to talk, the more she felt she couldn't marry this man. Princess Onika lost all hope of this being her destined future. Princess Onika had already fallen in love with Prince Ezra and what are the chances of him personally knowing her arranged husband? Princess Onika was not sure if this was a test of her loyalty or a sign that she and Ezra were meant to be together. As she looked at Prince Ramir, she knew that any Princess would be happy to marry him, but she couldn't help turn and look at Prince Ezra's face. As Princess Onika looked at Prince Ezra, she could see the pain in his face as a tear rolled down the side of his cheek. Princess Onika turned to Prince Ramir and whispered to him, "How do you know Ezra?" Puzzled by the Princess's question, he answered, "Ezra is my best friend. We grew up together. "As Prince Ramir replied, he looked at Prince Ezra and then looked into Princess Onika's eyes; he knew something wasn't right. The minster requested the exchange of the rings, when Prince Ramir took Princess Onika's hand to place the ring on her finger, he couldn't ignore her shaking hand. Prince Ramir softly caressed the Princess's hand and repeated his vows. With a suspicious smile, Prince Ramir reassuringly whispered to the Princess that the hardest part was almost over. Princess Onika's heart began to beat even faster as the minister gave her the ring to put on Prince Ramir's hand. So many thoughts raced through the Princess's mind, "Best friends! How can I get over Ezra if they're best friends? How can I be in love with my husband's best friend? This will be a disaster no matter what! If I don't marry Ramir, there's no guarantee I can marry Ezra. If I marry Ramir, I will be continuously tortured every time I see Ezra! If I shame my family, no Prince will ever want to marry me! I'm running out of time. What do I do?" The minister cleared his throat to regain Princess Onika's attention. Princess Onika slid the ring half way on Prince Ramir's finger, took a deep breath and began to say her vows as her voice shook and cracked. Suddenly, Princess Onika paused than she removed the ring from Prince Ramir's finger. Princess Onika looked to the minister and Prince Ramir. Then in a slight whisper, she said she needed to be excused. Princess Onika looked back down the long aisle, then turned to her left and right to find the closest exit and began walking to the door. Queen Cecilia instantly followed after her daughter as King Mateo addressed Prince Ramir's parents to ensure them that he would take care of the situation.

As King Mateo entered the room where his wife and daughter were, before he could get one word out, Queen Cecilia said, "Stop. Don't say a word and look at our daughter." The King replied, "Fine, but remember this is our tradition and I promised Onika's hand in marriage to Prince Ramir's father and I am a man of my word. If Onika doesn't get out there and marry Ramir soon I don't know if I can fix this and this action will bring shame to our kingdom," King Mateo said. As Queen Cecilia continued to try and calm their daughter down, she requested the King give them a few minutes alone.

As King Mateo walked back to the ceremony, he apologized to Prince Ramir's parents for the confusion. King Mateo convinced them that his daughter was overly excited and extremely nervous. The Queen shared that she was the same way at their marriage ceremony many years ago. Prince Ramir's father replied that if the Prince and Princess did not marry on that day there would be no marriage ceremony for Ramir and Onika later.

Queen Cecilia tried to give some encouraging words to Princess Onika but nothing seemed to help. The Queen hugged her daughter close to her heart rocking the Princess in her arms and caressing her hair, trying to assure the Princess that everything would be all right. As the Queen stopped rocking the Princess, she softly raised the Princess's chin to meet her eyes and said, "I saw the Prince from the festival among the guests." The tears fell even heavier from Princess Onika's face to confirm Queen Cecilia's assumption. "Dear Onika, what have you done?" asked the Queen. Princess Onika cleaned her face and asked to speak with Prince Ramir in private. Princess Onika said, "I have to speak with him before I go through with this marriage."

Prince Ramir was embarrassed and began to get frustrated with the delay and confusion. He excused himself to another vacant room on the opposite side of the exit where Princess Onika was. Prince Ezra didn't know what to do; he wanted to check on Princess Onika and then he wanted to explain the situation to Prince Ramir. Prince Ezra decided to stay seated and not add any more commotion to the ceremony.

Queen Cecilia walked back into the ceremony in search of Prince Ramir. She was directed to the room where he waited. The Queen notified the Prince of her daughter's request to speak to him in private. Prince Ramir agreed and entered the room where Princess Onika awaited him.

Prince Ramir: *Hello*

Princess Onika: *Hello, I'm sorry for all the confusion. I have to tell you something before we go through with the marriage ceremony. I met Prince Ezra eight months ago at my kingdom's annual festival celebration and we continued to see each other after that for about three months without my parents' knowledge. Nothing physical ever happened but we fell in love with each other*

Bri Jones

in the process. When I told Prince Ezra I was to be married in the following three months, we agreed not to see each other again. This is the first time we've seen each other since then. If you don't want to go on with the ceremony I understand, but if you do, I will go through with it.

Prince Ramir: *What do you want to do? Either way this is not going to end well, because he is my best friend. If we marry, this will cause a problem in our friendship and if we don't marry, the results will be the same. I haven't seen Ezra in several months because I've been doing so much training in preparation for our marriage.*

Princess Onika: *It's my fault because he didn't know of the ceremony until the last day we saw each other.*

Prince Ramir: *This was years of decision making for our parents to arrange this ceremony and a lot is at stake. We both made promises to our parents and kingdoms and it's our responsibility to uphold it.*

Princess Onika: *Do you think we will ever fall in love with each other and be happy?*

Prince Ramir: *It's not about us falling in love; it's about us making the best team in running our kingdoms and respecting each other as we grow. If we do fall in love then that will be a plus. I must excuse myself now and I will wait for you shortly for*

24

the continuation of the ceremony.

Princess Onika was not too happy to hear the response from Prince Ramir. She could not see a happy life with him nor anything close to what her parents shared.

As Prince Ramir entered back into the vacant room, he requested the presence of his friend Prince Ezra right away. When Prince Ezra entered the room, he saw Prince Ramir pacing back and forth across the room; at this point he knew Princess Onika told Ramir the truth.

Prince Ezra: *Ramir, I'm so sorry I truly didn't know or I would have never let things get that far.*

Prince Ramir: *I don't need your apology; I just need your promise. I'm going to marry Princess Onika today and you need to stay away from her. Don't try to do anything to jeopardize this wedding or our marriage.*

Prince Ezra: *How can you still go through with this knowing how we feel about each other? As my best friend, you can't seriously be considering marrying her. I would never do that to you. If you are willing to marry Onika after knowing that I am truly in love with her, then it's clear to me that you are no true friend of mine. You don't love her; you're only worried about your pride and your image.*

Prince Ramir: *The truth is both of our parents agreed that we would be the best fit for each other and we both intend to uphold that honor.*

Prince Ezra: *I have to be honest with you, I want to marry Princess Onika but if she wants to marry you then I won't stand in the way today or thereafter.*

Prince Ramir: *Then it's settled. This friendship is over! You need to leave now!*

Prince Ezra: *Understood, bye.*

Prince Ezra exited the room; he didn't go back through the ceremony doors. He went down a hallway that led straight to the room where Princess Onika was. Prince Ezra lightly tapped on the door while he slowly opened it and whispered, "Princess Onika, can I come in?" Prince Ezra didn't hear a response, so he continued to creep into the room looking around. Prince Ezra spotted Princess Onika asleep in a long chair. It looked like she cried herself to sleep. Prince Ezra kissed the Princess's forehead and softly called her name to wake her. As Princess Onika slightly opened her eyes, Prince Ezra smiled and kneeled beside her and confessed his love for her and assured her that he never stopped thinking about her and that he would like her to be his wife. He promised he would never stop loving her or leave her side again. Princess Onika smiled and replied, "I want to marry you too!" The Prince and Princess embraced each other closely.

Princess Onika: *How are we going to do this?*

Prince Ezra: *I'm here. We can make the announcement together.*

Princess Onika: *I think you should leave the ceremony and let me handle this part alone, because I don't want to add more shame to my parents and kingdom with rumors of scandal.*

Prince Ezra: *I understand, but we should both tell Ramir together. I can't let you do that alone. There is a hallway we can take to go straight to where Ramir is without going through the ceremony doors.*

Princess Onika: *Okay.*

Ezra knocks on Ramir's door with Onika by his side. Ezra didn't give Ramir a chance to say anything before he opened the door. When Ramir saw Onika and Ezra together, he already knew what they were there for. Onika apologized repetitively, but Ramir did not want to hear it. Ezra tried to redirect Ramir's anger away from Onika. Ramir blamed them both for humiliating him in front of all their guests. Ramir told them that they were a disgrace and a mockery to all respected kingdoms and their historical traditions. Ramir couldn't stand to look at either one of them anymore. Ramir left the room and then excused his parents from the ceremony as they left the building.

Onika begged Ezra to leave so she could speak to her parents in private, because his presence would only make things worse. Ezra didn't want to leave Onika to face her parents alone, but he agreed. Ezra didn't go far, but he assured Onika he would return to her kingdom within eight weeks to allow things to calm down.

Onika's parents noticed the commotion from Ramir and his parent and decided to look for her. Onika saw her parents in the hallway as she was walking back. Onika informed her parents of her decision not to marry Prince Ramir. They both were very disappointed with Onika's decision, but King Mateo was livid. Onika assured her parents she would make the announcement to the guests.

Princess Onika entered into the ceremony and made her announcement that she would not be marrying Prince Ramir and expressed her sincere apologies   After all the delays, there was not much shock left to the guest. Everyone left the ceremony and went their separate ways. Princess Onika exited the ceremony and instructed her chauffeur to take her back to the palace. By the time King Mateo and Queen Cecilia got outside, Princess Onika had already left. It was a long but quiet ride back to the palace.

Once the King and Queen entered the palace, the Princess had already changed her clothes and was waiting for her parents in the dining hall. Princess Onika knew she was going to have to face it sooner or later, so instead of hiding from this lecture, she decided to face it head on. The King was so frustrated he couldn't talk; he went straight to his room and requested not to be disturbed. The Queen sat with the Princess and explained how the King was feeling and how her decision affected everyone involved. The Queen reminded the Princess of the King's love for her and assured Onika that in time he would come around; however, she needed to be patient. "It's been a long

day for everyone. Let's make it an early night,"
suggested the Queen. The Princess agreed and went to
her room.

CHAPTER THREE

During the following several weeks, the King did not interact or say much to the Princess. The palace and kingdom were also very quiet in an attempt to minimize any additional aggravation to the King. The Princess never experienced this type of treatment from her father and it made her feel very uncomfortable. The Princess decided to take a long ride on her favorite horse, Gazel, to clear her mind and get away from all the tension. As the Princess rode her horse outside the kingdom of Zalaya, she found herself in unfamiliar territory and the view was incredible and peaceful. In front of her were miles of beautiful terrain, filled with colorful trees, flowers and animals walking freely throughout. A river that flowed so serenely and clear waters that mirrored the blue sky divided this beautiful terrain. The Princess lay in the grass looking up at the sky; she couldn't help but feel peace in her heart and spirit. This was exactly what the Princess needed. As the day drifted away, the Princess started her journey back to her kingdom knowing she would return to the beautiful terrain the following day.

After visiting with the elders of her kingdom she began her journey to the beautiful terrain, but on this day she decided to go pass the Pearl River, where she and Prince Ezra used to meet. As Princess Onika arrived to the Pearl River, from a distance she saw Prince Ezra! As Princess Onika got closer, she jumped off her horse and ran into Prince Ezra's arms. The two embraced each other closely and neither wanted to let the other go. Princess Onika began to tell Prince Ezra about how everything was going in her kingdom, which didn't seem to get any better and her father still was barely speaking to her. The Princess didn't realize her decision would have such a lasting negative impact on her relationship with her father and the kingdom. Prince Ezra tried to comfort the Princess, but he had to tell her about what was going on in his kingdom as well. As a tradition, the Prince's father speaks to the father of the Princess chosen to wed the Prince. It was not respectable for a Prince to approach a King for his daughter's hand in marriage directly. Prince Ezra asked his father if he would speak to King Mateo on his behalf for Onika's hand in marriage, Prince Ezra's father quickly declined after learning the details of the circumstances. Prince Ezra's father forbid him from pursuing Princess Onika any further because he did not want to cause anymore damage between the three kingdoms. When Prince Ezra told his father he couldn't do that, his father replied that he would not inherit the kingdom and he would need to leave the kingdom. As Princess Onika looked into Prince Ezra's eyes they both knew they were on their own and would never be accepted by their kingdoms. Prince Ezra and Princess Onika decided in three days they would leave their kingdoms and start their life together somewhere else.

Over the next three days, not much had changed around the palace or kingdom for Princess Onika. She was sad to leave her parents and the kingdom like this, but she knew it was her only key to true happiness. Princess Onika discreetly packed several of her things and hid them under her bed for her departure that evening. Before the Princess went to bed, she located her mother within the palace and embraced her strongly. Princess Onika told her mother she was sorry and expressed how much she loved her and father then went off to bed.

At midnight, while everyone within the palace and kingdom slept, Princess Onika fled. As the Princess got everything saddled onto Gazel, she rode off to meet Prince Ezra at their secret location. Once the Princess and Prince met, they began their journey together far away from both of their kingdoms. Throughout the night they passed through several small villages, none of which felt like home to them. They also wanted to avoid settling in a small village where any citizens would recognize them as royalty. Early afternoon, they entered into a small village named Nirvana, where the people were dancing, singing and having a good time. Nirvana was the most beautiful place they had ever seen. As they got off their horses to walk around, it reminded them of the festival when they first met. The citizens of the village were very kind and welcoming to Prince Ezra and Princess Onika without knowing their true identities. Instantly, they both felt this was the place for them, so they agreed to give the Nirvana village a try, plus they were very tired from their long journey.

CHAPTER FOUR

As they settled into the village, they promptly inquired about having a small marriage ceremony. The Nirvana citizens were excited and honored to host the unity of Ezra and Onika's love. Everyone agreed to set the wedding for that evening. Onika and Ezra were separated as she went with the women and Ezra went with the men of Nirvana to prepare for the ceremony. While the men arranged for the ceremony, the elder men shared their advice for having a happy and successful marriage. The elder women also shared their stories and encouraging wisdom for having a long and happy marriage to Onika. Ora, a highly respected woman of Nirvana, brought her own wedding dress and offered it to Onika to have. The wedding dress that Ora presented to Onika was handmade and designed by her deceased mother and it was very dear to her heart. Ora was so moved by Ezra and Onika's love for each other that she wanted Onika to have it. Onika was honored that Ora offered her such an exceptional gift; it warmed her spirit. Onika tried the dress on and it was a perfect fit; she looked flawless. Onika wore the hairpin and earring she received from her parents, because they were still very special to her. While Onika finished preparing for the ceremony, some of the women put the finishing touches on the decorations.

As Onika walked down the aisle she couldn't believe her eyes. Everything looked incredibly beautiful and this time she was excited to say her vows to her future husband. Onika couldn't stop smiling as she walked down the aisle. As a few tears ran down her face, she knew they represented the joy and happiness she felt as her daydreams were now a reality. As Ezra watched Onika walk toward him, he too shared in the excitement and happiness in his heart through his smile and tears. After exchanging their vows, Ezra and Onika shared their first kiss as husband and wife.

Back at the palace, Queen Cecilia realized Princess Onika never returned from her routine activities that evening. Often times when Princess Onika would leave the palace to start her day, no one would see her leave; however, when Onika's day concluded, the Queen would either hear or see the Princess when she returned. As night approached, Queen Cecilia began to worry and notified the King of her concerns. They both went to check Princess Onika's room and nothing looked alarming. So then they checked with the servants to find out if anyone had seen Princess Onika all day, and no one was able to provide any assistance. The King ordered the guards to begin searching for Princess Onika. The guards searched day and night for several weeks, but they were unsuccessful; Princess Onika was not found. The Queen missed her daughter very much and this created more tension between the King and Queen. The Queen began to blame the King for their daughter being missing. The Queen prayed that wherever her daughter was she was safe, happy and that she would see her again.

One year later, Onika gave birth to twins a beautiful baby girl named Athena and handsome baby boy named Elijah. Ezra and Onika continued to raise their children in the Nirvana village. As Ezra and Onika watched their beautiful children grow into young adults, they knew they made the right decision. Even though Onika and Ezra no longer lived in their kingdoms, they still raised their children with certain traditions, ethics and other values. They instilled in their children that they were special and to always follow their hearts.

CHAPTER FIVE

One afternoon, Onika told Ezra she was ready to go back to Zalaya to see her parents and let their children meet their grandparents. Onika felt their children were old enough to understand the choices they made and decide if they want to meet their grandparents. Ezra agreed to go back to Zalaya, but he had no desire to return to his former kingdom. Ezra missed his younger brother, but he knew his father would not welcome him back so easily. Onika had no idea how her parents would react or if they would accept her choices and family. Onika and Ezra shared their true identity and life story that led them to the Nirvana village with Athena and Elijah. Athena and Elijah were excited to hear about their heritage and did not regret being raised outside of the palace and far from Zalaya. Athena and Elijah loved their home in Nirvana and the family they grew to know, but they shared a curiosity in meeting their grandparents. The following evening during a dinner gathering, they announced to their friends of their journey out of

Nirvana and they were unaware of when or if they would return. As the sun rose, they said their farewells and started on their way. Onika had mixed feelings; she could imagine her mother being delighted to see them in spite of her abruptly leaving many years ago, but wasn't sure how welcoming she would be. Onika was very apprehensive as to how her father would react to her return, especially since she married Ezra. Onika prayed her father would accept her and their family and this would be a peaceful reunion for everyone. As night grew deeper over the sky, they decided to rest in a village not far from the Zalaya kingdom and continue their travels in the morning.

When Onika and her family entered the Zalaya kingdom, the guards at once recognized Princess Onika and rushed to her side to escort them all to the palace. When they entered the palace, the servants and guards shouted, "The Princess is home! The Princess is Home!" Queen Cecilia heard the shouting but couldn't understand what they were saying as she walked into the main hallway. As the Queen saw Onika standing there, she began to cry, "My prayer has been answered!" The Queen embraced her daughter tightly and didn't want to let her go. The Queen was so happy to see her daughter that she did not realize anyone else was in the room. After Onika and the Queen paused from their emotional reunion, Onika began to formally introduce her mother to her husband Ezra and their twins Athena and Elijah. Queen Cecilia was so overwhelmed; she didn't know what to say. So many years had passed since she had seen Onika that now she's a wife and mother of two young adult children. Queen Cecilia embraced everyone and welcomed them to the family. Queen Cecilia advised the chefs to prepare a big feast in honor of the return of Princess Onika and family while they sat in the social room. Two of the servants gave Athena and Elijah a tour around the palace, while they talked. Onika asked her mother where her father was, Queen Cecilia sadly informed Onika that her father was very sick and he was not in a mobile condition. Onika was saddened by the news but requested to see him. Queen Cecilia warned Onika that he was asleep and it would be best not to wake him at this time. Queen Cecilia directed Onika to the room where he was resting. Onika saw her father laying there from a distance; she couldn't imagine ever seeing her father like that.

Dinner was prepared and they all gathered around the table to talk about everything they experienced over the past several years. The Queen shared several stories about the Princess when she was growing up; Athena and Elijah really enjoyed learning more about their mother's childhood. As Onika was reminded of her childhood stories, she often glanced at her daughter because she could relate many of them to Athena. Hours had passed and it was getting late. The Queen requested that Onika spend some private time with her while everyone else got ready for bed. Onika gladly accepted, after she hugged and kissed her family goodnight. Queen Cecilia and Onika sat on the giant rug that was placed in front of the fireplace in the family room. This is where the Queen and Princess would snuggle up and talk when the Princess was younger. The Queen expressed her concern about the King's condition and the possibility that he would not be around for much longer. In addition, the Queen was not sure if the King would accept seeing Onika and the family because he was still very bitter about the disappointment of the ceremony and her abruptly leaving the kingdom. The Queen assured the Princess that the King loved her, but he struggled to express it because he was still very stubborn. The Queen asked the Princess if she would consider moving back to the Zalaya kingdom and leading the kingdom with Ezra. Before the Princess could answer, the Queen guaranteed that due to the King's illness, the Queen had to take full charge of the kingdom. So there was nothing King Mateo could do to prevent them from leading the kingdom. The Queen suggested that it would not be rushed, but the Zalaya kingdom needed a leader that cared about the citizens and possessed the vision to help Zalaya to continue to grow successfully. The Queen requested that the Princess sleep on it and discuss it with Ezra before giving a hasty response; Onika agreed. Onika did not want to lead the kingdom. She grew to love their life in the small village of Nirvana and she did not want her children to be faced with the pressures and traditions she had to deal with as a young adult. However, Onika did not want to let the citizens of Zalaya down. Torn with this hard decision, she decided to rest and discuss it with Ezra in the morning. Queen Cecilia reminded Onika that she didn't need her answer right away; she could take her time.

As morning came, Onika decided to tell Ezra about the details of the conversation she had with her mother that night. Surprisingly, Ezra was very supportive with either decision because he knew how much the Zalaya kingdom meant to Onika, as well as being close to her parents, even though the King was not as receptive. Ezra always was supportive of Onika's decisions, but was also honest about his feelings and thoughts, too. After Onika and Ezra talked it over, they decided to discuss it with Athena and Elijah to get their input. Athena and Elijah were both excited to learn more about the kingdom that their mother was raised in and also get to know their grandparents. However, Athena and Elijah shared mixed emotions about leaving the only home and friends they knew in the village of Nirvana. The village of Nirvana was not close to the Zalaya kingdom, it was almost a two-day journey. Onika still did not finalize her decision to lead the Zalaya kingdom, but she did want to move back to be closer to her parents.

As time passed, Athena and Elijah became very comfortable with the citizens of the Zalaya kingdom and lands that surrounded the kingdom. Athena and

Elijah also continued to build a strong relationship with their grandmother, Queen Cecilia. Onika and Ezra took Athena and Elijah to their secret meeting place and to the beautiful land by the river Onika found many years ago. Athena and Elijah enjoyed the different expeditions on which their parents would take them, but were more favorable with their own excursions. During many of Athena and Elijah's excursions they would meet several people their age from different kingdoms and villages. There was one young lady who captured Elijah's eye; her name was Kaamil. Kaamil and a few others friends would join Athena and Elijah on different expeditions and activities outside the kingdom.

One afternoon, Queen Cecilia requested to speak with Onika in private to inquire about her decision to lead the Zalaya kingdom. Onika denied the opportunity to lead the Zalaya kingdom; she felt it was not in her spirit or in the kingdom's best interest due to the challenges of the past. However, Onika suggested that Elijah and Athena lead Zalaya together until one of them decided to get married. Onika continued to declare that she would not impose the same traditional ceremony on her children that made her leave Zalaya. Onika wanted her children to have the opportunity to decide whom they marry or if they want to follow the traditional marriage ceremony of Zalaya. Onika convinced Queen Cecilia to help her support Elijah and Athena in their leadership role. Onika also suggested that Elijah and Athena would be great leaders, because they had grown to love and respect the Zalaya kingdom the same as she once did. Elijah and Athena both were very intelligent and wise beyond their years. Athena and Elijah returned to the palace from one of their adventures outside the kingdom with their friends. Queen Cecilia, Onika and Ezra sat down with them to discuss the opportunity to lead the Zalaya kingdom one day. Queen Cecilia explained the responsibilities and liabilities that came with being a great leader. Onika and Ezra promised Athena and Elijah that they would support whatever decision the twins made and told them to take as much time as needed to decide. Elijah knew right away that he wanted to be King of Zalaya when he began interacting with the citizens and learning about the structure of the kingdom. Athena did not share the same feelings as her brother, even though she loved the citizens of Zalaya and her new

friends, she still anticipated returning to the village of
Nirvana one day. Athena missed her friends and the
family she grew to know in Nirvana. While Athena did
not share the same desire to lead the kingdom of
Zalaya, she still wanted to experience the training with
her brother, Elijah. During dinner Queen Cecilia was
happy to discuss the destiny of the Zalaya kingdom that
would reside with Elijah, and his preparation to begin
training toward becoming King.

Due to Elijah's intensive training, he did not get a
lot of free time to see Kaamil and his other friends.
Elijah requested to take one day off to see his friends,
primarily Kaamil. Elijah explained to Kaamil his
decision to become King and his desire to marry her
and make her his Queen. Kaamil was happy to hear
that Elijah felt the same way for her that she did for
him. Elijah asked Kaamil if she would join his family
for dinner the following day; she accepted. Elijah met
Kaamil outside of the kingdom the following day to
escort her to the palace. As they entered the palace,
everyone was gathered around the table anticipating
their return. Elijah introduced Kaamil to everyone and
they greeted her with welcoming arms. Kaamil began

visiting the palace often for brunch and dinner since Elijah was so busy with training to see her outside the kingdom. The family grew fond of Kaamil's warm spirit and upbeat personality. One evening as they all finished dinner and brief conversations; Elijah announced that he and Kaamil wanted to marry and he would be visiting her family the following day. There was a short pause, but no one was too surprised by the announcement since the two had been spending so much time together. However, they knew every kingdom did not share in the alternative option to arranged marriage. Queen Cecilia spoke up to ask Kaamil if her parents knew of their plans or would they find out tomorrow? Kaamil replied, "We plan to announce it to them tomorrow and we were hoping you could join us." Onika and Ezra suggested properly meeting with Kaamil's parents before announcing their marriage plans. Onika went on to further explain her concern about Kaamil's family's views on marriage and traditional arrangements. Kaamil replied that her parents don't follow the strict traditional arrangements; she is allowed to be part of the final decision of selecting her husband. Onika and Ezra were slightly relieved to hear that. Queen Cecilia asked Kaamil,

"What are your parents' names?" Kaamil replied, "King Ramir and Queen Soma." Onika's heart dropped and reluctantly asked, "What is the name of your kingdom?" Kaamil replied, "The kingdom of Ashi." Ezra closed his eyes, turned his head and took a deep breath. Onika and Ezra didn't have to ask. They already knew Kaamil did not tell her parents who they were. Onika suggested, "I'm sorry, this might not be a good idea." Elijah and Kaamil did not understand why it wouldn't be a good idea. Ezra and Onika took Elijah and Kaamil into the family room to further explain the situation that occurred which would make unity so challenging. As Onika explained the history they all shared with Kaamil's father, Ezra grew very irritated and suggested that Elijah and Kaamil should stop seeing each other because, "Ramir and I will never see eye to eye again." Elijah and Kaamil pleaded with Onika and Ezra not to give up on them because they truly loved each other and wanted to be together. Ezra still had a lot of unease and mixed emotions toward Ramir. Onika suggested, "Maybe we should take a few days to collect our thoughts before pursuing any further actions." Onika requested that Kaamil wait a couple weeks before telling her parents and she should

49

return for dinner that day to discuss anything additional.

CHAPTER SIX

Later that evening, Onika went to King Mateo's room to watch over him while he slept. King Mateo made it obvious to Queen Cecilia that he did not want to see Onika or the children. Queen Cecilia tried to compromise with the King but there was no getting through to him and his condition was not improving. Onika disregarded King Mateo's demands by coming to see him while he slept. Onika couldn't help but to feel she was particularly to blame for the King's severe illness. Queen Cecilia knew she had to persuade the King to reconcile with Onika by using other resources. Normally it took two people, in addition to the Queen, to care for the King. The King was not the easiest person to care for, so when Queen Cecilia offered the nurse and assistant a temporary break, they did not hesitate to accept. Queen Cecilia would spend hours daily by King Mateo's bedside when she didn't have to cater to the demands of the kingdom. As a result of Queen Cecilia relieving the help, she requested Onika's help in caring for the King. Queen Cecilia made Onika responsible for feeding the King. The King declared that he didn't need Onika's help because he could feed himself. Onika got frustrated, so she placed the tray in front of him, and then sat in the chair by the window to wait for her mother to excuse her. The King began to feel helpless because he could barely hold the utensil steady to get the food in his mouth without making a mess all over himself. As a result, he knocked the tray over to the floor and refused to eat. Queen Cecilia responded, "If you don't let Onika help you, then you won't eat." It hurt the Queen to say that to her husband but she couldn't stand to see their relationship continue on this path. Usually, Queen Cecilia would sit with the King after she completed his routine care until he fell asleep, but instead she instructed Onika to stay. King Mateo guaranteed them he didn't need Onika to stay because he would rather be alone. The Queen did not give him the option for negotiation as she left the room. Onika followed her mother's instructions but did not attempt to start any conversation; she just stared out the window. King Mateo and Onika sat in complete silence until King Mateo drifted off to sleep. Queen Cecilia notified the kitchen staff that all food must be prepared and given to Onika only. As expected, a couple hours later the King requested a snack directly through the kitchen intercom. Onika returned to the King's room with his food and he quickly declared he lost his desire for food. The King knew he was hungry but his bitterness would not let go. "This is hopeless and I can't do this," Onika said as she stormed out the room.

The Queen entered the room and asked the King, "Why are you doing this to Onika? Haven't you lost enough time without her? Do you wish to make her suffer or even grow to hate you? You know Onika has the warmest heart, spirit and you know she loves you very much and seeks your forgiveness. Onika wants to rebuild the relationship you both once shared. Why deny her or yourself of that? You should be ashamed of yourself, our only child! Did you ever think if you didn't shut her out after the ceremony so quickly and maybe been a little open minded Onika would have never left?" Queen Cecilia continued, "I was hurt and angry about the situation also, but I love our daughter too much to treat her like an enemy. I'm just happy she returned in good health and happy. You're not going to have peace unless you're willing to let go of a grudge that happened decades ago. As the Queen continued to speak, the King would not look in her direction and remained silent. The King tried to ignore everything the Queen was saying but couldn't help hearing every word. Queen Cecilia walked over to the King's bed and kissed him on his cheek. Before leaving the Queen told him, "I love you and Onika very much and it breaks my heart to see you two not end this feud, if not for yourselves, please reconcile for me. Onika will be up shortly with your dinner."

The Queen persuaded Onika to return to the King's room, apologize and not to give up, just remain patient. As Onika got to the door of King Mateo's room, she took a deep breath and entered. King Mateo was so hungry from not eating all day; he didn't dare reject his dinner. Onika was slightly relieved, but she knew it was because he didn't eat all day and she was sure he had a big appetite. Even though Onika sat next to King Mateo's bed to feed him, he would not acknowledge her with any eye contact. After the King finished his meal, Onika remained seated next to him instead of sitting by the window or leaving. Onika just sat in the chair humming his favorite song from when she was younger until the King fell asleep. A couple days later Onika decided to break their silence.

Onika apologized for going against King Mateo's rules to see Ezra, lying to her family and also for bringing shame to him and the kingdom. Onika also expressed that she did not regret her decision to leave Zalaya to marry her love, Ezra, and start a family. Onika told the King that he gave her no other choices to obtain her happiness. King Mateo looked at Onika with resentment, and then responded, "What choice did you give me waiting until the wedding day to tell the truth about your secret Prince? You disgraced, shamed and embarrassed me and the Zalaya kingdom in front of everyone. Words can't express the anger I felt and part of me was glad you left and hoped you never would return."

Onika was shocked by the words she just heard come out the King's mouth. Tears began to race down Onika's face, with pain in her heart. "You were never concerned with my happiness or what was best for me. You were only concerned about having a strong legacy through Zalaya and monopolizing the other kingdoms by joining with the next powerful kingdom in Africa.

You portray yourself as this loving King and father but you are full of greed and are heartless. My happiness was never a factor for you; you're a liar. All those speeches about picking the best husband for me and my happiness were lies. You only showed love for me when I followed your commands and the first time I challenged your decision and followed my heart, you dismissed me like an annoying pest. I grew up living for your approval and to always make you proud but for what, for you to treat me like this and not even want to meet your beautiful grandchildren. I no longer need or want your forgiveness because I'm at peace with myself and I forgive myself."

King Mateo interrupted Onika's rant and reminded her that he was still her father and the King. "You will not speak to me in that manner or tone. Get out now!" he said.

Onika abruptly walked toward the door and replied "As you wish, you don't have to worry about me ever coming back to see you again." She slammed the door behind her.

Onika told her mother about the argument and

refused to return to King Mateo's room, especially since he stated he was hoping she would never return to Zalaya. The Queen tried to explain to Onika that her father was still angry, hurt and didn't mean what he said. He's just talking out of frustration. The Queen informed Onika of his concern and reaction when they discovered she was missing. "King Mateo never stopped praying for your safety and for you to return," the Queen said. She stated that the King was not happy with her decision, but he still loved her. "The King regrets being so strict and demanding, because he feels that's why he missed so many years of your life," she said. The Queen agreed that Onika should not return to the King's room for now, to give him time to cool off and also evaluate what was said to Onika. The next day, Queen Cecilia was accompanied by the nurse assistant to care for the King. The Queen did not mention that she was aware of what happened the previous day. The Queen conducted herself like nothing was wrong. King Mateo was hesitant with his words, since Onika did not return; he knew the Queen knew something. He didn't want to create more tension with his wife, so he kept quiet. By the second day, King Mateo asked where Onika was. The Queen looked at the King and asked. "Would you like to see Onika?" The King replied, "I was just asking to see if she was still in Zalaya." The Queen never gave a direct answer but replied, "When you're ready to see her,, I will send for her." King Mateo remained silent. As the Queen was getting ready to leave, the King softly requested for Onika to bring his dinner. The Queen humbly agreed. When Onika returned to the King's room, she was so nervous because she didn't know what to expect. Onika sat in the chair next to her father's bed then placed the tray on the table. There was complete silence as she fed her father; she could tell he wanted to say something, but he didn't seem sure how. Onika didn't want to attempt to break the silence again since the last time was a disaster. After the King finished his meal, Onika remained in the chair in silence.

The King cleared his throat and in a cracking voice said, "I'm sorry." The King attempted to clear his throat again and repeated "I'm sorry, Onika; I never meant to put so much pressure on you and make you feel like I wasn't proud or loved you; the truth is you bring me great honor just being your smart, intelligent, strong-minded and warm-hearted self; I couldn't ask for a better daughter. I should have listened to you instead of demanding you to do something I thought was best for you. I should have been open minded to realize what worked for your mother and me, is not guaranteed to work for you. I was heartbroken when you left and blamed myself for losing you and I never forgave myself. Will you forgive me?"

Onika jumped out of her chair and embraced her father closely. "I forgive you and I'm sorry, too. Please forgive me, she said as tears continued to run down her face. King Mateo embraced Onika as tightly as he could. "Yes, I forgive you," he said. King Mateo and Onika didn't want to let go as they continued to embrace each other and shared tears. Onika found herself lying next to her father with her head resting on his chest as they shared laughs and stories. As time passed, Queen Cecilia quietly peeked into the room and realized they had settled their differences. The Queen made her way over to embrace them both with a great big smile, then left them to catch up. Hours passed as they both fell asleep. The sunrise woke Onika up, so she snuck down to the kitchen to surprise her father with an early breakfast. When Onika returned to the room, her mother was kneeled down by the King's bedside sobbing with her head resting on his hand. Onika realized her father's eyes were still closed and he was not responding. Onika dropped the tray and ran over to her mother's side. The Queen embraced Onika and told her, "You both made your peace, so now his spirit can rest." The rest of the family and the kingdom were notified of the news of the King. Later that evening the kingdom hosted a ceremony in honor of King Mateo.

CHAPTER SEVEN

Elijah and Athena had soon completed the intensive leadership training and Athena felt it was time for her to return to Nirvana. Athena had so many great ideas to introduce to the Nirvana village, she couldn't wait to return. Athena did not want to waste any time, so she said her farewells to the Zalaya citizens and the friends she made from outside the kingdom. Onika decided to accompany Athena because she did not feel comfortable with Athena traveling alone. Onika decided to ask Queen Cecilia to join them, because Onika felt she would benefit from the visit. Queen Cecilia accepted. Ezra remained at the palace with Elijah to assist with additional training requirements. The following two days the ladies began their journey to Nirvana. When they arrived to the village, the citizens greeted them with a warm and loving welcome. Queen Cecilia was amazed on how beautiful the terrain was and how energetic the citizens of Nirvana were. The citizens prepared a large dinner to celebrate their return. Of course, the citizens realized

Ezra and Elijah did not accompany Onika and Athena. Athena addressed their absence at dinner and announced she was the only one from her family that was going to reside in Nirvana. Athena informed the citizens that her relatives sent their regards but had other obligations to uphold.

After a day of rest, Onika and Athena took Queen Cecilia on a journey through Nirvana and the surrounding area. Queen Cecilia never imaged anything so beautiful; she felt like she was in a different world. Everything was so peaceful and calm. Queen Cecilia never felt so relaxed and liberated. Queen Cecilia looked as all the beautiful colors from the sky reflected on the river. As Queen Cecilia stood there; she felt the calm breeze revitalizing her skin and running through her hair. Queen Cecilia felt free like a young child. Queen Cecilia had no worries or concern as she became one with nature. Right then, Queen Cecilia had a new respect and understanding for Onika's free spirit. Queen Cecilia was never adventurous or spontaneous. As a young Princess, Queen Cecilia never ventured outside her kingdom to the country sides of Africa. Queen Cecilia was always restricted to the kingdom yard unless she was traveling with her parents. Queen Cecilia also had three siblings that she was very close with and they kept each actively entertained in the palace growing up. Onika and Athena enjoyed watching Queen Cecilia gain the same appreciation and experience from the place they both grew to love. Queen Cecilia returned daily to the same area, often walking along the terrain or simply laying in the field watching the sky as time passed gracefully.

As Athena began to get settled, Onika advised her on how to structure and introduce her ideas to avoid being overbearing, aggressive, or brutal. Queen Cecilia also advised Athena on remaining humble, patient, understanding and open minded to alternative suggestions. Athena was grateful for her mother and grandmother's guidance and support. Since Nirvana was a small village they did not have a traditional ruler; however, they had Senior Officers who made decisions on behalf of Nirvana. Athena asked the Senior Officers to hear her ideas and visions she had for Nirvana. The Senior Officers accepted. That afternoon, Athena conducted a presentation of her thoughts and mission for the growth, strengthening and success of the

Nirvana village. While the majority of the Senior Officers were excited and welcoming of the new ideas Athena was presenting, there were a few Senior Officers who were very challenging. Athena was secure in the success of her vision and opportunities it would make available to Nirvana. Athena remembered what her mother and grandmother advised her and she was able to respectfully restore confidence in the doubtful Senior Officers. Onika and Queen Cecilia were very proud of how Athena conducted herself and kept her composure even when things became challenging. The Senior Officers of the Nirvana were so grateful for Athena's genuine love and sacrifices that she was making for the village. To show their gratitude, the Senior Officers asked Athena to honor their village as the first Queen of Nirvana. Athena gracefully accepted. The Senior Officers and Onika assisted Athena in selecting a strong support team to help create and make her vision a reality. The Senior Officers and citizens officially voted Athena, as Queen of Nirvana and the ceremony would be held the following days. Onika and Queen Cecilia remained in Nirvana after the ceremony to assist Athena in getting more acquainted with her new position as Queen. Onika was happy and felt reassurance that Athena would be fine without her as she watched Athena master her responsibilities. The next morning, Onika and Queen Cecilia started on their way back to Zalaya. Onika knew she still had to face the situation with Elijah and Kaamil.

CHAPTER EIGHT

O nika arrived to the palace after her long trip from Nirvana. Surprisingly, Kaamil was already at the palace visiting Elijah. Onika wasn't ready to entertain the reality of their situation; she was tired and just wanted to rest. Onika knew she couldn't postpone it much longer. As they gathered around the table for dinner, Elijah decided to mention the possibility of meeting with Kaamil's parents to discuss their marriage arrangement. Onika could see how in love Elijah and Kaamil were with each other. Onika could see the same love she shared with Ezra resembled in Elijah and Kaamil. Onika knew that "no" was not an option for them either. It disturbed Onika because she wasn't sure how this union would take place without any conflict. Onika recognized that Ezra hid his guilt and hurt from losing a close friend by exhibiting anger. Onika could only conclude that Ramir felt the same way, plus Ramir was rejected at the altar and humiliated in front of everyone. Onika feared for the worst, but prayed for a miracle. Onika could still see the displacement of rage in Ezra's eyes when Kaamil said who her father was. Ezra tried to show his support during dinner, but he struggled with his feeling of guilt and anger toward Ramir. Ezra tried not to say much, but when he did everyone could feel the tension in his voice. Onika suggested the three of them have dinner with Kaamil and her family. Onika and Ezra agreed it would be better for Kaamil to be honest and upfront with her parents rather than surprise them. Ezra predicted that Ramir would not go forth with the dinner, let alone the marriage, because of the history they all shared. Onika tried to persuade Ezra to meet with Ramir first, to try to reconcile their differences. Ezra abruptly declined and insisted that would never happen. "It's Elijah and Kaamil who want to get married. I'm not forcing or stopping them, so it's not about me," said Ezra. There was brief silence at the table. Kaamil responded, "I will speak with my mother first in hopes of gaining her support, then talk to both of my parents together."

Kaamil waited until the next morning to speak with her mother alone, while her father was out with her brother. Kaamil told her mother that she needed help convincing her father to approve the marriage.

Queen Soma was not sure how that was going to happen because she was also familiar with the history and hatred King Ramir had toward Ezra and Onika. Queen Soma knew that even waiting until King Ramir was in a great mood wasn't guaranteed to help because just a mention of either name brought rage to his eyes. Kaamil expressed to Queen Soma, that there were no other option. She was going to marry Elijah. Queen Soma insisted Kaamil use a more submissive approach with her father. Queen Soma also volunteered to speak to King Ramir first on Kaamil's behalf. Kaamil happily welcomed her mother's assistance. Later that evening King Ramir and their son, Tobias, returned. Queen Soma decided to discuss Kaamil's proposal with King Ramir in private. As expected, King Ramir was outraged and refused to compromise. Queen Soma tried to calm him down but he was not receptive. King Ramir called for the servants to bring Kaamil to the room right away. As Kaamil entered the room where her parents were talking, Queen Soma pled with King Ramir to hear Kaamil out. King Ramir began to pace the room in frustration.

Kaamil cried out to her father, "I'm in love with

Elijah, and I want to marry him. I can't help who his parents are. Please don't try to keep us apart." Kaamil had always kept a soft spot over her father. King Ramir replied, "Baby girl, there has to be somebody else who could bring you more happiness than Elijah. Isn't there someone who doesn't have so much tension between the families?" Kaamil insisted there was no one else for her but Elijah and pleaded for King Ramir's approval. King Ramir replied, "I'm sorry, baby girl. At this time, I can't give you my approval because I don't want our family to have anything to do with them. Elijah is from a family that has no honor or loyalty. Honestly, I don't want you seeing him anymore." Kaamil replied serenely, "I love you, dad, and I'm going to marry Elijah. I just want you to accept it without hostility." King Ramir stared at Kaamil in shock by her response and then turned to walk out the room. Queen Soma asked Kaamil to be patient and not to do anything impulsive. Queen Soma went after King Ramir and said, "I don't want to lose our daughter. This feud between you and Ezra is not worth breaking up our family."

The next morning Kaamil convinced Queen Soma

to go with her to Zalaya while King Ramir and Tobias were out for the day. Kaamil felt if her mother met Onika and Elijah, it might help. When they arrived to the Zalaya palace, Kaamil formally introduced Onika and Elijah to her mother. Ezra was assisting Queen Cecilia in a meeting with some of the citizens of Zalaya. Elijah and Kaamil went to the kingdom yards so their mothers could talk in private. Onika told Queen Soma about the choices she and Ezra made when their parents tried to keep them apart. Onika feared that the same could happen with Elijah and Kaamil. Queen Soma agreed and shared the same fear. They both knew the hardest part would be to convince their husbands to accept the marriage without vengeance.

Queen Soma and Kaamil arrived back to the Ashi palace before King Ramir and Tobias returned. When King Ramir and Tobias returned, Queen Soma and Kaamil requested King Ramir to accept Elijah, Onika and Ezra to dinner for the following evening. King Ramir was unenthusiastic about the idea but eventually agreed. Without hesitation, Kaamil quickly ran out of the room to send a messenger to officially invite them to dinner before King Ramir could change his mind.

As Kaamil returned to the room, she jumped into her father's arms with a big smile as she thanked him. Queen Soma looked to King Ramir and smiled. She knew this was a step in the right direction.

Onika felt a sense of relief when she received the dinner invitation from the messenger and accepted. Onika brought the invitation to Ezra and Elijah. Onika and Elijah both held their breath while they waited for Ezra's response. Ezra stood still with a skeptical look on his face, and then he finally accepted. Onika and Elijah both embraced Ezra as they thanked him. Onika wasn't expecting a quick fix but felt hope because things were now going in the right direction.

Onika, Ezra and Elijah arrived to the Ashi palace. Onika encouraged Ezra to remember that this was in support of their son's happiness. Inside the palace, King Ramir received the same message in reference to Kaamil from Queen Soma. As everyone gathered around the table, King Ramir and Ezra remained civil. Queen Soma and Onika led most of the conversations at dinner. King Ramir and Ezra barely spoke and tried to avoid making eye contact with each other. This was the first time they had seen each other since the dreadful marriage ceremony. Everyone could feel the tension brewing between King Ramir and Ezra. There was a brief silence at the table, and then Kaamil expressed her excitement about planning the wedding ceremony. King Ramir replied, "I hope Elijah doesn't have any envious best friends who will try to sabotage the ceremony." Ezra laughed and said, "I knew it was coming; you're so arrogant and stupid to realize the world doesn't revolve around you. No one cares about you, but you and you're too selfish to realize that. I don't know how many times I have to say it but *I Did Not Know Until I Saw Onika Walking Down The Aisle*!" King Ramir replied, "You were always spiteful of me and tried to compete with me over everything and that was just one more thing."

Queen Soma and Onika both tried to calm their husbands down but the men just got louder with rage. Onika decided it was time to leave as she pulled on Ezra's arm. Queen Soma told Kaamil to walk them out while she attended to her father.

Queen Soma pulled King Ramir into another room and shut the door to detain the yelling. Queen Soma told King Ramir, "This was not the time for that. You and Ezra need to work out your differences before the wedding because this outrageous behavior can't happen again." King Ramir responded, "I'm not going to the wedding; you can stand for me." Queen Soma replied, "You can't mean that; it will break Kaamil's heart if you don't walk her down the aisle." King Ramir said, "I'm not stopping the wedding; that should be enough, plus Kaamil made it clear she was going to marry Elijah either way. I have nothing else to say about it."

Elijah began to get frustrated with his father's behavior. Elijah recalled Ezra's remarks about how prideful and stubborn Ramir was, but Elijah began to see those characteristics in Ezra. Elijah started to have empathy for King Ramir's feelings of betrayal by his best friend running off with his intended bride. Elijah knew that it was not intentional, but the mortification Ramir felt in front of several families, friends and respected figures of different kingdoms was understandable. Elijah felt King Ramir's anger was justified. Elijah decided to speak up and asked his father to apologize to King Ramir for unintentionally humiliating him on his wedding day and mocking their friendship. Elijah expressed to Ezra the results of his prideful ways and the logic of humbly apologizing for his part in ruining their friendship. Ezra tried to justify his position, but the more he listened to Elijah, Ezra knew Elijah was right. Ezra decided to walk back into the palace and apology to Ramir. Onika, Elijah and Kaamil remained outside. Ezra felt even if Ramir did not accept his apology, his spirit would finally be at peace. Ezra saw Queen Soma and King Ramir still speaking in the foyer of the palace. Ezra modestly interrupted their conversation and asked to speak to Ramir in private. Queen Soma excused herself and let them speak in private. King Ramir was first resistant to hearing anything Ezra had to say.

Ezra didn't know where to began, but he knew he truly missed his best friend. Ezra respectfully told Ramir, he was sorry for the embarrassment he caused him and walking away from their friendship for so many years. Ezra further explained how he missed their friendship. Ramir accepted Ezra's apology. Ramir apologized for blaming Ezra for intentionally sabotaging the wedding and their friendship. Ezra accepted. Even though Ezra and Ramir could never get back the many years they lost, they both felt a sense of peace. They embraced each other and then Ezra left the palace. When they arrived to the Zalaya palace, Onika and Elijah expressed their gratitude to Ezra for reconciling with Ramir.

CHAPTER NINE

The day before the wedding the Zalaya kingdom hosted a celebration in honor of their soon to be King and Queen. The celebration lasted all afternoon. The citizens performed a parade that consisted of drums, dancing, singing and other entertainment. Elijah and Kaamil enjoyed the celebration activities and visiting with the citizens to show their appreciation. Queen Soma attended the festivities alone, because King Ramir did not feel comfortable going. Onika kept Queen Soma company during the festivities and showed her around the terrain. Onika and Queen Soma shared in conversation over their excitement for Ezra and Ramir's reconciling their differences. They both felt their families were moving in a positive direction. As the celebration came to an end, Elijah escorted Kaamil and Queen Soma back to the Ashi palace safely.

The trumpets filled the air throughout the kingdom of Zalaya as the sun ascended in the sky. Queen Athena arrived just in time to join her family for

Bri Jones

breakfast before the marriage ceremony. Onika happily updated Athena about Ezra and Ramir reconciling their differences. Athena was surprised, but happy to hear the news. Athena shared the success of her projects being implemented throughout Nirvana. Everyone was proud to hear about Athena's accomplishments. They continued to share laughs and enjoyed some memorable moments before preparing for the ceremony.

As Queen Soma helped Kaamil get ready for the marriage ceremony; she gave Kaamil a pair of earrings that she was given on her wedding day from her mother. Kaamil was proud to wear them. Queen Soma shared some encouraging words and memories of her wedding day with Kaamil. King Ramir and Tobias were also getting ready to attend the wedding. Even though King Ramir accepted Ezra's apology, he still felt uneasy about going to the wedding. Tobias was not happy about going to the wedding at all. Tobias idolized his father; in his eyes King Ramir did no wrong. He lived for King Ramir's love, approval and acceptance. Tobias felt Ezra and Onika were the reason why King Ramir's reputation suffered and disagreed with his father's decision to accept Ezra's apology so quickly. King Ramir and Tobias put their feelings aside to show their love and support for Kaamil's happiness. They both knew how important it was to Kaamil for them to be there.

King Ramir walked Queen Soma and Kaamil out to their carriage as he complimented them on how beautiful they looked. King Ramir embraced Kaamil and told her how much he loved her, and then he got into the carriage with Tobias. Kaamil was happy to have her father's support at the wedding. King Ramir and Tobias's carriage followed as Queen Soma and Kaamil's carriage led the way to the ceremony.

As they arrived to the ceremony, Queen Soma and Tobias were escorted to their seats. King Ramir and Kaamil were directed to a private room before the ceremony began. Onika greeted King Ramir and requested to speak with Kaamil in private. King Ramir waited outside the room to give them privacy. Onika told Kaamil how proud she was to be her mother in-law and gave her the necklace she wore during Ezra and Onika's wedding. Kaamil was honored to wear the necklace. They embraced each other, and then Onika proceeded back to the ceremony room. Kaamil was filled with joy to have all the people she loved there and getting along peacefully. Kaamil was most excited about marrying her true love.

Kaamil looked beautiful as she walked down the aisle in a gorgeous long white gown trimmed in gold flower print. Elijah watched as Kaamil walked closer toward him; Onika and Ezra had never seen him so happy. Onika and Ezra knew right then they made the right choice approving the marriage. After the wedding ceremony, the celebration event began. The celebration festivities lasted all night until the early morning. Elijah and Kaamil resigned back to the Zalaya palace to enjoy some alone time before the festivities ended.

The next morning Elijah and Kaamil prepared for the coronation ceremony, where Elijah would be officially crowned as King of Zalaya. Ezra agreed to be Elijah's advisor and Onika agreed to assist Kaamil in her role as Queen. Queen Cecilia would also oversee Elijah and Kaamil in their roles. Queen Soma was supportive and attended the coronation ceremony alone. King Ramir did not feel comfortable attending.

After the ceremony, they all gathered in the social room of the palace to continue their celebration.

CHAPTER TEN

Elijah and Kaamil decided to tell their families of Kaamil's pregnancy. Elijah and Kaamil kept the pregnancy from their families before the wedding, but Kaamil couldn't hide it any longer. Onika and Ezra had mixed emotions about the news, but they were excited about becoming grandparents. Queen Cecilia was disappointed, because this would bring dishonor to the Zalaya kingdom. King Ramir and Queen Soma were not excited about the news, but were accepting. King Ramir was disappointed because he knew this would generate more humiliation for his family. Tobias immediately blamed Elijah and became outraged with him. Tobias felt Elijah took advantage of his sister and was responsible for adding disgrace to his family's reputation. Tobias hated to see his father in distress and suffer more humiliation on the account of Ezra's family.

Tobias felt the only way to reclaim his family's reputation would be to defeat the Zalaya kingdom in war. Tobias felt the ongoing disrespect to his family had to end. Tobias was the chief over the Ashi military and took it upon himself to meet with the military to declare war on Zalaya in honor of his family. When Queen Soma learned of the plan of war against Zalaya, she demanded that it be called off. Tobias would not acknowledge his mother's commands. Queen Soma pleaded with King Ramir to end the war before it started. King Ramir refused to order Tobias to withdraw from the war. Queen Soma argued that King Ramir would regret it.

When King Elijah received the message that the Ashi kingdom was declaring war on Zalaya kingdom, he tried to contact the Ashi palace without any success. King Elijah did not want to go to war with Ashi, but he knew he had to protect Zalaya. Queen Cecilia was not surprised by the news. She felt it was going to happen either by the direction of King Ramir or Tobias sooner or later. Queen Cecilia had seen wars start from disagreements, family humiliation and less significant situations. Onika and Kaamil were outraged with the news and sent messengers to Ashi palace in efforts to reach Queen Soma, which all failed. Queen Kaamil attempted to go to Ashi to speak with her brother directly, but King Elijah was against it. King Elijah felt it was too dangerous and didn't want her involved in a stressful situation.

Ezra was infuriated when he heard the news and immediately organized a meeting with Zalaya military. Ezra was very familiar with the structure and organization of the military because he was chief over his kingdom's military as a Prince. Ezra provided King Elijah with detailed strategic plans for orchestrating the military for attack and protection. Ezra also informed King Elijah that they needed support from outside military kingdoms to ensure Zalaya's victory. Ezra suggested King Elijah stay by Queen Kaamil's side and let him handle it. Ezra felt the absence of King Elijah and the war would be overwhelming for Kaamil during her pregnancy. King Elijah trusted his father and knew he needed Ezra's guidance, so he gave him full authority to make decisions on behalf of the Zalaya military. As authorized by King Elijah; Ezra sought assistance from Nirvana through a messenger. Ezra also wanted the help from his former village, but he knew he would have to make that request in person. Without delay Ezra left for his former kingdom alone.

Ezra had not been to his kingdom nor seen his family since his argument with his father. Ezra knew his chances were slim, but it was worth the effort. Ezra arrived at the gate of his former kingdom and requested to speak with the King. Ezra notified the guard who he was and the guard escorted him to the palace. Ezra knew he had to be humble and accept whatever his father had to say. The King walked into the room where Ezra was waiting, except the King wasn't Ezra's father. It was Ezra's younger brother, Omar. Ezra stood to his feet to embrace his brother, but Ezra only received Omar's hand. Ezra could feel the tension from his brother and knew this was not going to be easy. Ezra and his brother were really close growing up, especially after their mother passed away. Ezra asked his brother where their father was.

King Omar: *Dad died 10 years ago. Why are you acting like you care now? What do you want? Why are you here?*

Ezra: *Honestly, I need help from your military. Ashi has declared an outrageous war against Zalaya.*

King Omar: *You have some nerve. You haven't thought about us enough to come visit or make sure we're okay in decades. But now you need help so you want to act like you never abandoned our family. Wow, you are so heartless and selfish. You were my big brother and I looked up to you, then you just walked away and never looked back. Now I'm supposed to drop everything because you need help.*

Ezra: *I'm sorry I never came back, but I didn't want to face dad. We never really got along. I do regret not being strong enough to at least come visit you, but I always checked on you through other sources. I'm sorry I wasn't here for you; I never stopped missing you and our friendship. I knew I was not going to receive a warm welcome coming here, but I'm in need of support from your military.*

King Omar: *Even if I wanted to help you, which I don't, it would not be in the best interest for our military to get involved or show support in this war against Ashi. Everyone can figure out this is a personal feud with no bases.*

Ezra: *Understood. It was good seeing you again and I wish you well.*

King Omar: *The guards will show you out.*

Ezra knew it would take time, but he knew he had to rectify things with his brother. Ezra regretted not making the opportunity to reconcile with his father before his death. Ezra promised himself that he wouldn't let the same thing happen with his brother.

After the war and when everything returned to normal; Ezra planned to make every effort to repair their relationship. When Ezra returned to the Zalaya palace he was reluctant to tell his son that they would not receive help from his former kingdom. King Elijah was not surprised, but did receive word back from Queen Athena that several citizens of Nirvana were volunteering to fight with Zalaya. The volunteering citizens of Nirvana were preparing to arrive to begin training with the Zalaya military. King Elijah was nervous, but he knew he could not demonstrate any fear; instead he displayed confidence in Zalaya military's victory over Ashi. Ezra knew it would be a challenge to defeat the Ashi military, but as long as the Zalaya military remained focused and executed the strategic plans, they could be victorious.

Once the Nirvana volunteers arrived, Ezra conducted a meeting with all the military to review the tactics and approach. Ezra knew they did not have any time to waste and he did not want to give Ashi the opportunity to overpower Zalaya by a sneak attack on the actual kingdom grounds. Ezra knew he was dealing with a more experienced military so he didn't want to take anything for granted. Zalaya kingdom was less experienced because they were not frequently involved in war in comparison to other kingdoms. Most kingdoms did not challenge Zalaya to war, because they were such a valuable asset for their products, services and other supplies.

Ezra planned to lead the military outside the perimeter of the Zalaya kingdom at nightfall. Ezra knew this would keep the citizens a safe distance away from the battlegrounds. Onika was not enthused about Ezra being on the battlefield; she felt it was too much of a risk. Onika tried to convince Ezra not to go and let the chief of the military handle it, but Ezra made his decision final. Ezra said farewell to his family and assured them he would return safely. Onika and Ezra embraced each other tightly after sharing a passionate kiss, and then Ezra whispered to Onika, "I will return." Ezra then began to lead the military out of the kingdom in search of a location they could setup. Ezra did not want to go to battle with Ashi, but he knew he couldn't surrender either.

Ezra set up a secure perimeter outside of Zalaya kingdom to prevent any Ashi militant from getting through. Throughout the perimeter, each Zalaya militant was paired in small groups, which were located out of plain sight. The Zalaya militants were instructed to attack any Ashi militants who tried to infiltrate without hesitation. One person in each group was responsible for staying alert while the others rested to avoid an ambush.

As morning came, Ezra checked on each group and verified there were no Ashi militants. Ezra decided at nightfall, he would relocate the Zalaya militants closer toward the battle line. This would give them a better view of the Ashi militants when they arrived. As the sun rose the following day, Ezra was surprised to hear no one had seen or heard any activity from the Ashi militants.

The Zalaya militants began to chant victory over the Ashi militants because they never came to battle. Ezra encouraged the Zalaya military to stay focused because this could be part of their enemy's plan. Ezra knew there was going to be a battle; he just wondered about what strategy they were using. Ezra decided not to move the Zalaya military any closer to the Ashi kingdom line because that could be a trap. Ezra also knew he had to keep his militants focused, because Ashi could be waiting for their guards to be down to attack.

Before night fell, Ezra met with all the militants and assured them this would probably be the night of attack from the Ashi militia. Ezra warned the Zalaya military that Ashi was preying on their ignorance, so stay vigilant. There was no indication of the Ashi military all throughout the night.

During the early morning before sunrise, Ezra heard the first sound of the Ashi military. Ezra discreetly alerted the Zalaya militants to hold their positions and get ready for attack and defense. Ezra could see that Zalaya had more militants than Ashi, but he didn't underestimate their skills. As the actual fighting began, Ezra directed his small group on a different path. Ezra had navigated a path that could put them behind the Ashi military to execute an ambush. Waiting for the Ashi military to arrive for battle, Ezra studied and became familiar with the terrain, learning of secret paths and layouts.

With the help of his small group of Zalaya militant,

Ezra was able to lead in the capture of Ashi's military chief, Tobias, during a surprise attack. Ezra knew with this leverage, he could finally end this war and hopefully prevent any future disputes. Tobias was sent to the Zalaya prison for holding until Ezra could negotiate some terms with King Ramir. Ezra had no intentions of hurting Tobias, but he couldn't let King Ramir know that. King Ramir was notified of Tobias's capture by the Zalaya military.

King Ramir already felt the guilt of losing his relationship with his daughter, Kaamil; he couldn't imagine losing Tobias, too. King Ramir directly ordered Ashi military to withdraw from battle. King Ramir sent a messenger to request the words of Ezra's demands in exchange for the safe release of Tobias. Ezra required King Ramir to sign a peace treaty agreement to permanently stop hostility now and in the future between Ashi and Zalaya kingdoms. King Ramir agreed to Ezra's demands and in return Tobias would be released in three days back to his kingdom of Ashi.

Queen Cecilia was impressed by Ezra's tactics and ability to lead the Zalaya militants to victory. Onika was happy to see Ezra and King Ramir both signed the peace treaty. Onika was mostly proud of Ezra, for his great honor and tactics in restoring peace to Zalaya. In spite of Tobias's unmerited actions, Onika still wanted the families to resolve their differences and build a strong relationship. Onika was hopeful that Kaamil's pregnancy would help bring the families closer.

Queen Kaamil went to visit her brother while he was in Zalaya's prison. The guards allowed Queen Kaamil to enter Tobias's chamber, but they remained close. Queen Kaamil sincerely asked Tobias to end all his hostility toward her in-laws. Queen Kaamil told Tobias; if he causes anything to happen to her husband or in-laws, she would never forgive him. Queen Kaamil pleaded with her brother by expressing her love for him, her family, husband and unborn child. Queen Kaamil told Tobias of her desire for him to be a part of her life and her unborn child's life. Queen Kaamil told Tobias she didn't want to live without him in her life, but she wouldn't leave her husband either. Tobias promised his sister he would make an effort for her. Queen Kaamil and Tobias embraced then she left his chamber. Tobias awaited his release from the Zalaya prison the following day.

The afternoon of Tobias's release; Ezra accompanied the guards to Ashi kingdom. King Ramir and Queen Soma waited at the palace doors as they escorted Tobias. King Ramir and Queen Soma embraced Tobias and welcomed him home. King Ramir requested to speak to Ezra in private. The guards waited outside the palace. King Ramir thanked Ezra for keeping Tobias safe and he apologized for the grief that was caused. King Ramir commended Ezra on his admirable tactics. King Ramir assured Ezra that his gratitude for his children's safety has surpassed any hostility he once had toward him. Ezra humbly accepted King Ramir's apology. Ezra and King Ramir embraced each other.

As Ezra exited the palace doors; the guard notified him that Queen Kaamil was in labor. Ezra ran back into the palace to notify King Ramir and Queen Soma. Ezra suggested that they return to Zalaya with him. Ezra felt it would be great to welcome their first grandchild into the world together as a family. When they arrived to the Zalaya palace; Onika and King Elijah were in the room with Queen Kaamil and the doctor. Queen Cecilia waited in the palace foyer for them to arrive. From the foyer they could all hear Queen Kaamil's cries for her mother's presence. Queen Cecilia escorted Queen Soma to the room where Kaamil was. Kaamil was so happy to see her mother's face; she began to weep. King Ramir, Ezra and Tobias had no desire to go in right away; they decided to wait outside the room. Moments later the next sound that filled the Zalaya palace was the sound of a baby girl. Queen Cecilia peeked out the door and directed Ezra, Ramir and Tobias into the room. Kaamil was pleased to see her father and brother. They all took turns embracing and congratulating Queen Kaamil and King Elijah and greeting the baby. The excitement and joy they all felt subsided any thoughts of past aggression. Queen Kaamil and King Elijah decided to name their daughter Shalaya. This represented the love that united the Ashi and Zalaya kingdom.

The End